SUPER DAD

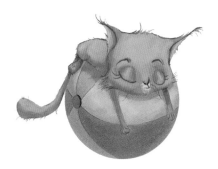

To Dylan

I wish you a 'Super' Christmas!

Wesley Ray

For all Super Dads out there.

Copyright 2020 by Wesley Fogel
Published by Wesley Fogel Publishing

Text copyright © Wesley Fogel 2020
Illustration copyright © Cristian Bernardini 2020
ISBN: 9798695375664

SUPER
DAD

Story by
Wesley Fogel

Illustrated by
Cristian Bernardini

Published by
Wesley Fogel Publishing
www.wesleyfogel.com

A little ant sits on a leaf
To have a power nap

He dreams of his dad
As a breathtaking bee
Who moves around with a zap!

With wings so wide and eyes so big
He flies around so fast

He fights off baddies
Left and right
His powers are unsurpassed!

A baby bee lays down her head
And sleeps to the pretty birdsong

She dreams of her dad
As a super strong spider
Crime fighting all day long!

With wiggly arms and extraordinary strength
His enemies are no match

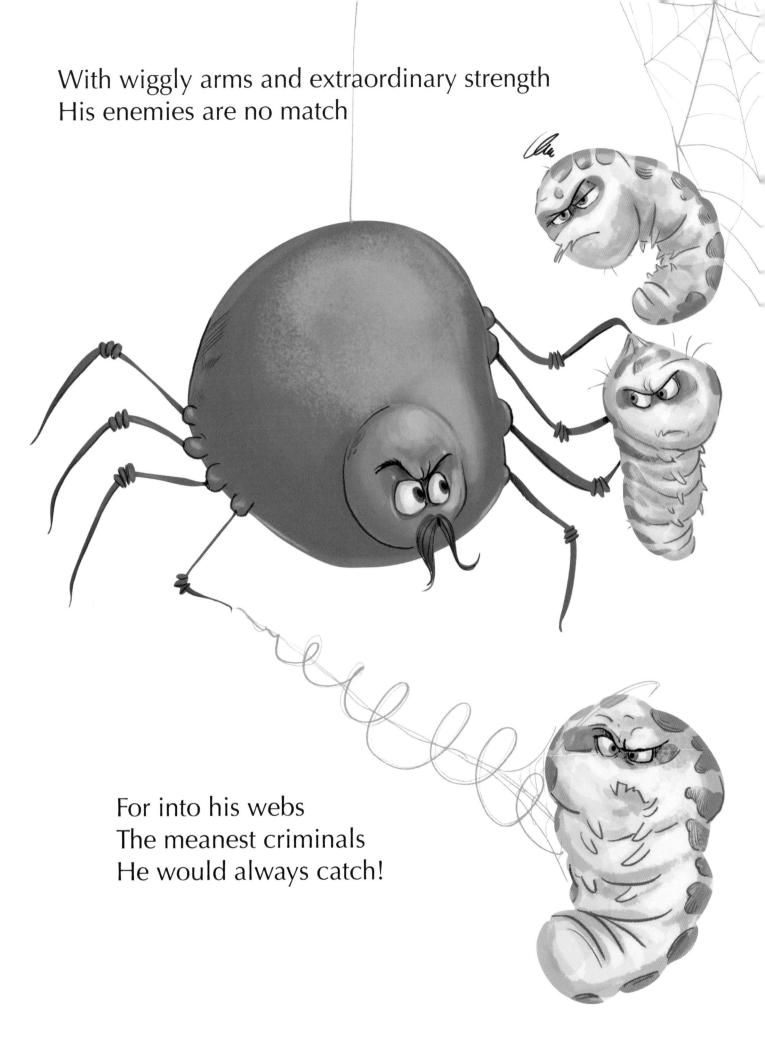

For into his webs
The meanest criminals
He would always catch!

A teeny spider slumps in his web
For a brief mid-morning rest

He daydreams of his dad
As a rip-roaring rabbit
On a magical super quest!

He hops over here, he hops over there
Nobody can be quicker

For if anyone tries to
Escape his reach
They wouldn't wait long for a whisker!

A soft baby rabbit snuggles up
For a nice little cozy doze

And dreams of his dad
As a courageous cat
Who wears the most splendid clothes!

His fearsome eyes and immensely high leaps
Catch the best of them off guard

If you cross this kittie
While doing wrong
Beware you might get scarred!

A little kitten on a ball
Drifts off for a catnap

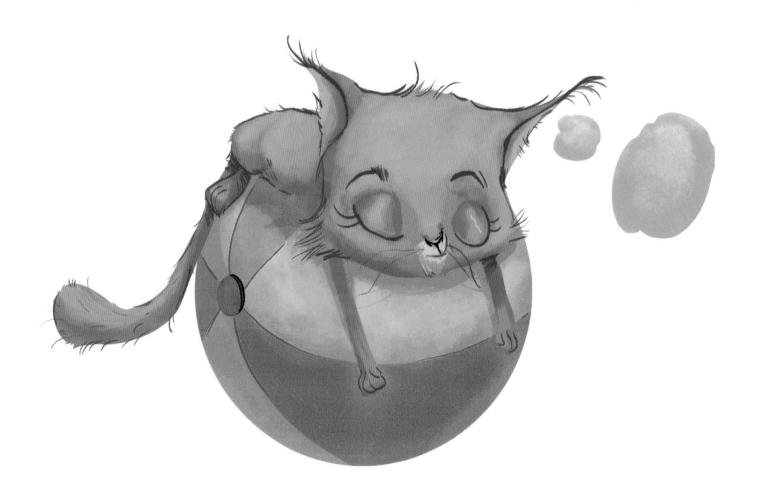

She dreams of her dad
As a lusty lion
Waiting for villains to trap!

With his long furry mane and humungous fangs
There were few who didn't fear

The fate of anyone
Who dared to strike
His victory was never unclear!

A baby lion lays down to rest
And catches forty winks

He dreams of his dad
As a remarkable rhino
Getting into more high jinks!

With a big broad neck and imposing chest
It is very hard to ignore

You can try to hide
When he comes at you
But you'll end up on the floor!

A baby rhino settles down
Into a gentle slumber

She dreams of her dad
As an enormous elephant
Who roams around with a lumber!

With his huge flapping ears and big long nose
His sheer size is most imposing

When you hear him stomp
You won't stay long
To receive a terrible hosing!

A baby elephant slips quietly off
For her lunchtime siesta

She dreams of her dad
As a great blue whale
Who acts like a movie star!

As big as the ocean he lands with a splash
And spouts water way up high

The only way
You can ever escape
Is in his tummy as a fresh fish pie!

You may be big
You may be small
But you'll always have your dad...

... To dream of giving super powers
And defeat anyone who's bad.

DRAW YOUR OWN SUPER DAD!